THE SEASHORE PEOPLE

ALSO BY CLIVE KING

Stig of the Dump
Ninny's Boat
The Sound of Propellers

THE
SEASHORE
PEOPLE

CLIVE KING

VIKING KESTREL

VIKING KESTREL

Penguin Books Ltd, Harmondsworth, Middlesex, England
Viking Penguin Inc., 40 West 23rd Street, New York, New York 10010, U.S.A.
Penguin Books Australia Ltd, Ringwood, Victoria, Australia
Penguin Books Canada Limited, 2801 John Street, Markham, Ontario, Canada L3R 1B4
Penguin Books (N.Z.) Ltd, 182–190 Wairau Road, Auckland 10, New Zealand

First published 1987
Text copyright © Clive King, 1987
Illustration copyright © Mike Daley, 1987

British Library Cataloguing in Publication Data

King, Clive
The seashore people.
I. Title
823'.914[F]   PZ7

ISBN 0-670-81723-6

Printed in Sabon
by Richard Clay Ltd, Bungay, Suffolk

For Emma the swimmer

CONTENTS

No, we are not seashore people, neither you who read this story nor I who tell it. We like to be beside the seaside, but the sea is a stranger to us and we cannot trust it or the food we find on its shore. But perhaps, a long time ago, a very long time ago, there were people who lived in the sea, and the land was as strange to them as the sea is to us.

I

FOOTPRINTS

Lisha went along the beach on her hands and knees.

'*Lisha . . . Lisha . . . Lisha . . .*' The little waves of the sea sang her name.

The beach was empty except for a gull standing on the wet sand. The sea was nearly calm. The sky was blue and the sun was very warm. The land was just a heap of grassy sand-hills at the top of the beach.

Lisha's hands made prints in the damp sand, and her knees and toes made tracks behind her. She came to a little river of salt water that was trying to get back to the sea. Her hands sank in the oozy sand. She scooped up handfuls of it, and slopped it into the bed of the little river. The water couldn't get past the heaps of sand, so it tried to get round. Quickly, she heaped up more.

Ouch! Her hand met something hard and sharp, buried in the beach. She pulled it out and looked at it – a big flat shell with ridges on it. She sniffed it. It smelt of seawater. Nothing to eat on it, just half a scallop shell. But it would do to dig with. She scooped up more damp sand and built up a wall.

The water was making a little pool behind it. More water kept trickling down the beach. Where was it coming from?

Lisha followed the little river up the beach, bringing her big shell with her. There were shiny damp pebbles, grey and red and yellow ones, and white ones that the light shone through. She chose the pebbles she liked, and put them in her shell. They looked pretty, but the warm wind blew on them and soon they were dry and dull. She threw them away, one by one, not into the sea but up on to the powdery sand.

Then she went up the beach to see where they had landed. *Ooh*, the sand was hot! There was a line of dead black seaweed, empty crab shells, sandy seagull feathers. Lisha stopped there. Beyond it the dry sand stretched up to the dunes. The wind sang a shivery song in the sharp-looking grasses. Lisha didn't like the dry part, away from the friendly sea. She felt alone on the empty beach.

But was she alone?

She could see a track in the sand, leading from the dunes to the edge of the water. Something had crawled out of the sea on to the land.

Or something had walked off the land into the sea!

Lisha scuttled down the beach, past her overflowing pool, and into the sea. She plunged her head down in the shallow water, where the breaking waves stirred up clouds of sand and floating seaweed. She always felt safer in the sea.

She lifted her dripping head from the water and sat up in the foam of the breakers. She wiped the salt water from her eyes, and looked across the bay to the rocks. Her family were over there. Perhaps she'd better go back to them. They didn't like her going off alone, towards the land.

But she had to know what made those tracks. It might have been a mother turtle, clambering up the beach to lay her eggs in the warm sand. Lisha liked eggs. She lay low in the water and let the current carry her along the beach.

There they were, the tracks! She let the rolling waves carry her on to the sand again. The strange footprints went right into the water, and the little waves were filling some of them in again. But in the firmer sand they were sharp and clear. Which way were they leading – into or out of the water?

Lisha squatted and looked at a print. Where had she seen something like that before? A row of toes and the sole of a foot?

The toes seemed to point to the sea. She turned and faced it, got up on hands and feet, and tried to fit one of her feet into the print on the sand.

'*Ha! Ha! Ha! Ha!*'

Who was that laughing at her? She looked up through her legs. Only a gull flying overhead. She made a face at it.

She looked down at her foot and the strange print.

The Seashore People

They fitted.

Her own footprint?

But she'd never been on that bit of beach!

She made another careful footprint alongside one of the strange ones. No, they weren't quite the same. Same size, same row of toes, same shaped sole. But she couldn't push her foot in as deep as that footprint went. Her print was faint and flat. That one was made by a foot that was firm and knobbly.

And beside her own footprints were her handprints, of course. Beside these strange ones – *there were none!*

Lisha didn't like it. Something without hands had walked into her sea! She galloped on hands and feet back into the water, and pushed through the breakers till she felt herself afloat. But she didn't feel safe any more. That *Thing* was in the water! She swam as fast as she could back towards the rocks and her family.

Oh, yes, Lisha could swim. Arms and hands were for scooping the water. Legs and feet were for flipping like fishes' fins. You breathed in air above the water and bubbled it out beneath it. Crawling about the beach was fun, but it made you tired. Swimming was easier, and faster.

Now the thought of food made her hurry. Something inside her told her that feeding-tide might be nearly over. Lisha knew that twice every day the rocks heaved themselves up out of the sea, and twice every day they sank back into it. Or so it seemed to the seashore creatures, anyway. When the rocks were high

14

it was picnic-tide. Had she missed it? She hoped her mother had saved her some food.

She swam to the rocks and let a big, slow sea-swell lift her on to them. There was her family, already settling down to their after-lunch sleep. Eating and sleeping – that's all they seemed to care for, Lisha thought. She was the only one who liked *exploring*. Her mother opened her eyes and moaned a bit, but Lisha was used to that. It meant: '*You'll never grow big and fat if you don't eat.*' Lisha's mother was sleek and plump like all the healthy seashore people. Her dark bronze skin and her long hair shone in the sun.

She had saved a pile of food for Lisha. Whelks and winkles. Lisha felt hungry when she saw them. There was a seagull's quill handy for picking them out, and she munched the salty, fishy little mouthfuls. But, left in the sun like that, some of the food was going off already. She let it go off. It crawled into the cracks in the rocks and back into the rock pools. *See you next lunchtide, winkles!* Anyway, she'd had enough.

An uncle and a couple of aunts were stretched out in the sun. So was her grandfather, Old Snoldge – but he always kept an eye open to see that there was no trouble in the family. Lisha's cousin Pilp was awake too, and so was her baby brother, little fat Swodge. Lisha didn't feel sleepy either.

She thought of a game to play: *two-feet*. Holding on to a rock, she got up on her own two feet. Dare she let go with her hands, and see what it felt like to walk on just two feet? Pilp was watching her. She would show him. She let go, and staggered forward. One step. Two steps! Pilp's eyes were round with amazement at this new game. Lisha's feet slipped on some damp seaweed and she sat down very hard on the rock. Pilp laughed, but it wasn't funny. There were sharp barnacles where she had sat down.

Of course Pilp had to have a go. He pulled himself up by a boulder, grinning. He let go with his hands. One step. Two steps. Three! But then he stumbled over a ledge in the rock and fell forward, bumping his head on a ridge. Grandfather Snoldge gave a stern bark. He didn't like these silly games on the rocks.

None of them had noticed that little Swodge wanted to play, too. He'd finished his meal of mother's milk and was clambering over Mummle near the edge of the rock. But he was going to stand up, like the others!

Splosh!

Lisha wondered what had happened. She looked over the edge. Down in the deep green water over the sand, there was little Swodge, his arms and legs waving like a crab's claws. Lisha called to Pilp and pointed downward. They both leaned over the edge and laughed at the funny sight.

Swodge bobbed to the surface. He was laughing too. The water didn't bother him – he'd been born in it and he was quite old enough to come to the top and breathe. But there was another cross bark from Old Snoldge. What was he worrying about now? Lisha saw that the current was carrying the baby out to sea.

She dived smoothly into the water and dragged her little brother back to the rock. Pilp heaved him out and humped him back to his mother.

From the water, Lisha beckoned with her finger to Pilp. They often went off together while the grown-ups were resting. Nobody minded, so long as they didn't go towards the land. But that was just what Lisha meant to do.

She had another game with Pilp first – *underwater hide-and-seek*. She took a deep breath, tipped over, pushed her legs up in the air, and swam down, down towards the sunken rocks and the waving seaweed. If you kept your eyes open underwater you could see the underwater world. It was wavier and hazier than the world above, but you could understand it if you were used to it.

What was that great creature down there?

For an awful moment Lisha thought of the *Thing* that had walked into the water. It was yellowy-greeny, with thin waving limbs that rowed through the water, and a hard humped shell, and a beak and foolish staring eyes. And it wasn't alone. There were other flapping things like it, in the green distance.

But it was all right. Lisha knew that creature who was staring at her. It was Mother Turtle. Lisha had met her before, and she was nothing to be afraid of. Lisha always kept clear of her horny snapping beak, but she sometimes used to tease her by tickling her back flippers.

Lisha went to the top again for another breath of

air. She laughed at Pilp who was staring around, looking for her. Then she dived straight down again. She had something to ask those turtles.

What was it, exactly?

Who walks on the land with two feet and no hands?

But when Lisha came to open her mouth the water got in. People can't talk under water. And anyway turtles don't understand.

Yet perhaps, in the underwater world, thoughts can float from mind to mind without words. For as Lisha stared at monstrous old Mother Turtle in the flickering under-sea light, this is the answer she seemed to get:

'*We are the Turtle People. We*
Began in the sea, for all things come from the sea.

We crawled on the land, and
On empty beaches buried our eggs in the sand.

They hatch in the sun
And for each tiny turtle its journey's begun

Back to the sea.
That's where we all want to be.'

And Mother Turtle flapped her way up to the surface of the water to take a breath. She hadn't breathed for half an hour.

Lisha followed her up. But Mother Turtle hadn't really answered her question, so Lisha tweaked her back flippers as they went up. She took a good look at those flippers. That *couldn't* have been Mother Turtle, walking on her hind legs on the beach! The idea was so funny that Lisha had to laugh. It's not a good thing to laugh under water. Lisha got to the top choking and spluttering, with salt water up her nose. And Pilp pounced on her. He had seen the bubbles coming up from her underwater laugh.

Lisha broke away from him and swam quickly towards the beach. Pilp was a fast swimmer too, and they got there almost together. Pilp wanted to play *tumbling-in-the-surf*, but Lisha swam with her head high in the water, looking out for those tracks. It was a long beach, and it wasn't easy to be sure of the right spot. And now there wasn't so much beach between the sea and the dunes.

Where *were* those tracks? Had she really seen them this morning?

There they were! Lisha let a breaking wave carry her to the beach. She felt safer, now that Pilp was with her. Yes, there were the footprints that had led into the sea. She called and beckoned to Pilp to come and look.

Pilp didn't like leaving the water, but he came in slowly through the surf. Lisha did what she had done in the morning. She faced the sea, got up on hands and feet, and put her foot into the strange print. Pilp looked at her, very puzzled.

She looked down at her foot. But there was something wrong. The toes were pointing the wrong way!

So she turned herself round, with her head towards the land. Her foot nearly fitted now. Yes, the prints were like the ones she had seen in the morning. But this lot led the other way.

The Thing-without-hands had walked out of the sea!

Of course Pilp had to try and fit his foot into the print too. Lisha giggled. He did look silly, balancing on his hands and feet with his bottom in the air! His foot made a mark like hers, but a bit smaller because he was younger. It wasn't like the strange footprint.

Lisha's eyes followed the track across the firm sand, over the tide line of dry seaweed and feathers, and on over the smooth sand towards the dunes. Then she saw something that made her grab Pilp by the arm and topple him over.

Up there! On top of the dune! Dark against the blue sky!

A figure that stood on two feet. It didn't only stand. It danced. It pranced. Its arms waved in the air. Was it waving at *them?*

Pilp and Lisha tumbled over each other as they scampered into the sea and swam as hard as they could back to the rocks.

2

SEABIRDS

Lisha dreamt that night about two-legged creatures. The first thing she saw when she opened her eyes next morning was a two-legged creature, staring at her with a round eye.

A bird.

What was odd, then, about walking on two legs? Millions of birds did it every day. She would go and talk to the birds about it.

It was a breezy day. Little white clouds blew across the sky, and little white waves danced on the sea. As soon as she could, she went and found Pilp. He was glad to come with her. Just as they were going to the edge of the rock to dive into the sea, they heard a wail behind them. It was little Swodge, wanting to come too.

Babies! Oh well, perhaps he could come to the stack and see the birds. The stack was not far from the rocks where the seashore people slept. But the stack belonged to the birds. It stood near the cliff, a tall pile of rock with ledges from top to bottom of it. Only birds could reach those ledges, or stay on them. The seabirds went there to lay their eggs and hatch their chicks.

Lisha had to cross the choppy bit of water to the stack with Swodge on her back, clinging round her neck. But she was used to that. There was a tumble of big boulders at the bottom of the stack, covered with seaweed and barnacles. The sea swirled among them, and the swell rose and fell. Pilp got himself on to a boulder. Lisha held the slimy stalk of a seaweed, as she wallowed in the swirling water with Swodge on her back, half choking her. Pilp was lying on his belly, trying to grab Swodge. He got him by the arm and pulled him off Lisha's back – but then he felt himself slipping, and let go. Swodge was washed away among the seaweedy boulders. Lisha went after him. This wasn't funny. They shouldn't have brought Swodge with them! She got hold of her baby brother just as a wave was going to dash him against a rough rock, and backed away into the open water again.

A seabird was sitting calmly on the water, looking at Lisha. It lifted its wings, gave a little push with its legs at the top of a wave and a flap of its wings, floated easily into the air and glided on to the rock where Lisha wanted to get. Treading water and hanging on to fat Swodge, Lisha felt cross with that bird. Showing off! Making it seem so easy! She could do that, if only she had wings.

She dragged Swodge round to where the water

washed up and down a slope of rock, green with fine thin weed. Pilp met them there, and helped haul Swodge up out of the water. They scrambled up away from the waves, and rested for a bit.

Lisha watched the clouds of birds soaring round the stack. One of them folded its wings in the air and dropped like a stone, beak-first into the sea. Where had it gone? There it was, popping up on the surface. It had a little fish in its beak. Cleverly, it twiddled the fish round so its tail was sticking out, then swallowed it. Lisha saw the bump going down the bird's throat. Would she like to eat her dinner that way?

Pilp had got bored with sitting there and was climbing higher up the rocks. Lisha wasn't going to be stuck there with Swodge, so she humped him along and followed Pilp. She didn't like climbing much. Barnacles and rough edges scratched her knees. Her toes felt for foot-holds, but they would rather be flipping through the water. Pilp had got on to a flat rock above her head. How could she get Swodge up there? She propped her back against the rock and stood upright – yes, she was standing, but the rock was holding her steady. She heaved little Swodge up in front of her, his face to her face, and held him as high as she could. Pilp leaned over from the rock above and hauled him up. Then Lisha had to find hand-holds and foot-holds to get herself up after them.

She needed another rest. She'd rather swim twice across the bay than do all this. A seabird hung on the air in front of them. The wind, blowing against the stack, was lifting it *upwards* past them, and it wasn't even flapping its wings. Was all this climbing worth the bother?

But Pilp kept going. He was edging round the stack on a ledge now, peering round a corner, waving to her and pointing excitedly. Lisha thought she could see a safer way round that corner, a bit higher up, along a broader shelf. Dumping Swodge in front of her at each move, she climbed up and along. They were higher than Pilp now, and she made a face down at him. Then she peered round the corner too.

And wished she hadn't! She was much higher than she thought. Below her, the rock went straight down to the dark, foaming sea. Round the corner she could see a great gloomy crack that went deep into the stack, from its top to its bottom. Upwards, both sides of the crack were lined with ledge after ledge, and birds were sitting on them. More birds flew at every level in and out of the crack, into the shadow and out into the sunshine. At the very top the dark rim of the crack almost closed round a piece of bright sky.

She watched Pilp try to throw a lump of loose rock across the great crack. He didn't throw hard enough and the rock fell down, down and plopped into the sea. The sound of the plop echoed against the walls of rock.

And then Swodge, on his tummy in front of her at the edge of the shelf, gave a little squeak and pointed with his fat finger. What was he pointing at? She put her head down to his. There, nearly close enough to touch, on a little ledge, was an egg and a fluffy ball – a chick. Swodge reached out to grab at them, and Lisha had to haul him back.

And – whether it was Pilp throwing the stone or Swodge trying to grab the egg that set them off – anyhow, the birds all at once burst into a screeching chorus!

'*Akkety-awk! Akkety-awk! Akkety-awk!*
Akkety-awk! Akkety-awk! Akkety-awk!
Akkety akkety akkety akkety akkety!
Awk! Awk! Awk! Awk! Awk!
Akkety-awk! Akkety-awk! Akkety-awk!'

Every bird on every ledge, every bird swirling round in the air – they all joined in. The noise bounced to and fro off the rock walls and couldn't get out. Lisha couldn't think for the noise. What was she doing here? She put her fingers in her ears. That was better. She had come to ask the birds something. What was it?

Oh yes. *How do you learn to walk on two legs?*

That was all she wanted to know. She shouted against the din of the bird people, but they didn't listen to her. So she listened to them. She didn't really understand bird-language, but the noise of it beat into her skull, and this is what it seemed to say:

'*We are the birds! We are the birds! We are the birds!*
We came from the sea, for all things come from the sea.

The Seashore People

We danced on the land, and our feathers grew.
We took to the air, and we flew! We flew! We flew!
Ages and ages before there were creatures like you.
We can dive in the sea, we can swim on the waves,
* we can walk on the land.*
We can dance in the air! The air! The air!
What can you do? Do? Do? Do?
Not even lay an egg! Ha! Ha! Ha! Ha! Ha!'

Lisha was fed up with the noisy, stuck-up birds. Why did they have to say everything over and over again – even if what they said was true? Had they answered her question? No. They just made it sound easy, dancing on two legs. But it wasn't.

Sometimes she wished she was *anything* except Lisha, one of the seashore people. And this was one of the times. She had to get down all those rocks, and take fat Swodge with her.

Swodge reached out again for the egg on the ledge – and a bird swooped down out of the air and flew at him, its sharp beak pointed at his eyes! Lisha pulled him back roughly and struck out at the bird. It flew off, laughing. Lisha backed off quickly along her shelf. This could get dangerous! The birds didn't want them there.

A bit below them, the birds were diving at Pilp on his ledge. Lisha needed Pilp's help to get Swodge down the rocks, but Pilp was too busy with the birds. They weren't really trying to peck Pilp's eyes out. They were swooping down and flying up at the last moment, bluffing. But they didn't care if they upset him off the rock and made him fall.

Then suddenly the birds weren't swooping round Lisha and Pilp and Swodge any more. All at once they lifted and poured like smoke upwards to the top of the stack. But the noise of their cries seemed louder than ever! What had happened?

Lisha couldn't see from where she was, so she humped Swodge back to the end of the shelf again, and looked up the crack. She could hardly see through the thick cloud of birds at the top of the crack. Their white feathers now looked black against the bright sky as they dived over and over again at the nesting ledges at the very top. But what were they diving at?

And then she saw, on the rim of the crack, dark wiry figures climbing lightly *downwards* from the top, on to the highest nesting ledges! Other figures, like them, danced and pranced against the sky, on the very rim.

They were all like the figure she'd seen on top of the sand-dune!

What could they be? And what were they doing up there?

Stealing eggs! That's what they were doing. The skinny egg-robbers were calmly standing on the ledges, lifting eggs from the scrappy nests and passing them up to figures above. And they seemed to be taking no notice of the screaming, wheeling birds.

Lisha looked down to Pilp, to make sure that he

had seen the same thing. He had. And he must have thought he could get away with eggs too. He was crawling along a narrow ledge towards some nests, reaching out for the eggs. *Greedy Pilp,* Lisha thought, *I wonder if he'll give me some?* Of course she liked eggs if she could get them, but she wasn't going along one of those ledges, even if the birds weren't there any longer. And anyway she had Swodge with her. But there was that nest near her. She reached out and grabbed the egg.

She held it to her ear and shook it. No, she liked fresh eggs, but she knew when one was too near hatching. This one had a chick in it – it might be tough. She put it back.

And she was glad she did! From right at the top of the stack, a mother bird had seen Pilp on her ledge with a handful of eggs, and come swooping down at his face!

He let go of the rock with his other hand to save his face – and toppled outwards off the ledge.

Lisha clutched her little brother and shut her eyes. If Pilp fell on to the sharp rocks below –

She listened for the thud of his body.

Splasssshhh!

He had hit the water. But even water can damage you if you fall from high enough. Lisha opened her eyes and made herself look down. She could see the bubbles of the splash, and Pilp's body coming slowly to the surface. He didn't seem to be moving. Had he knocked all the air out of himself?

Then she saw him shake his head and spout sea-water out of his mouth. He began to swim out of the dark water of the crack. He was all right.

But was *she*? She wasn't going to stay here. There were those strange creatures, up there on the same stack. She just wanted to get back to the home rocks. And she wasn't going to wait for Pilp to swim round, climb up again, and help her down with Swodge.

She had to manage it alone, balancing the baby on any flat place she could find, telling him sternly to stay put, letting herself down to the next footholds and heaving Swodge down after her. *Ooh*, she would never go climbing again – with or without a baby!

At last they were down on the safer boulders near the sea. And there was Pilp, looking a bit shaken. And empty-handed of course. But before she could get to him he was moving off round the bottom of the stack, waving madly to her to follow him and pointing to the top of the cliff.

She'd had enough of crawling over rocks. She plopped into the sea – it was lovely to have the water taking her weight! She settled Swodge on her back and swam round the stack to see what Pilp was pointing at.

What a sight! The stack was near the cliff – once it must have been joined to it, but the sea had eaten the bridge away. Now there was quite a gap between the top of the cliff and the top of the stack, though they were both at the same level. But what was going on up there?

The Seashore People

There was still a cloud of excited birds. But it was something else that made Lisha gasp. Those wiry figures, those egg-robbers – they were *leaping* across that dizzy gap, from the stack to the land. And they weren't using their hands, because their hands must have been full of birds' eggs!

What sort of creatures could they *be*?

Just then, Lisha didn't want to know. She turned round and swam back to the home rocks with her brother.

3

SEALS

Rain fell in the night. It was dry in the sleeping-cave among the rocks, but Lisha heard its pitter-patter outside and the swishing sound as it fell in the sea. The wind had changed, and it carried with it a singing sound in the early morning dark, the sound of unhappy voices, rising and falling.

When she left the cave it was still raining. It was cold, but Lisha liked the feel of the falling water on her naked skin. There were pools of water in the rocks, high above the sea. She tasted it. It tasted of – nothing! But she drank and drank. If you live in the water you don't get thirsty often, but this rainwater was a treat.

The cliffs were hidden in drizzling clouds. The rain beat the sea flat and made it look dull and grey. Lisha sat on the edge of the rocks and hugged her knees. It wasn't a very happy day.

There was a blob of white floating in the grey sea. It was slowly drifting towards the rocks.

'*Meeeeh!*'

The white blob had bleated! Now Lisha could see it had two dark eyes.

'*Meeeeh!*'

It was an unhappy little bleat. Almost a people sound, but not quite. Whatever was making it sounded lost.

Lisha slipped into the flat water and swam gently towards the thing. As she got nearer she could see clearly its big sad dark eyes and its little black nose. It was paddling hopefully towards her with a pair of flippers. No hands. It wasn't a little person. It had lovely white fur all over it.

Lisha stayed as still as she could in the water, and the little animal swam up to her and nuzzled her. Whatever it was, it was a baby. But a big baby, as big as Swodge.

'*Look, I'm not your mother,*' Lisha said. What was she going to do with it? She'd better take it back to the rocks.

She swam back slowly, and the baby animal followed, paddling easily with its front flippers and flipping with its back ones. No feet either. This wasn't the thing that had made tracks in the sand – and it certainly couldn't climb a stack.

Lisha's mother was watching from the rocks as she got back, with the baby following.

'*What is it, Mummle?*' Lisha asked her mother. You could ask your mother *simple* questions like that, and get a simple answer. But for the difficult questions – well, there didn't seem to be the words.

Seals

'*Seal*,' said her mother.

'*What does it eat?*' Lisha asked.

'*Fish*,' said her mother. She turned away to look after Swodge. But she was smiling. She didn't mind Lisha playing with the baby seal.

Pilp came to the edge of the rock to have a look. Lisha put her finger to her lips. She didn't want Pilp to make a noise and frighten the seal, perhaps by jumping in with a splash.

'*Fish!*' she called to Pilp, and pointed to the seal. He might be able to catch a fish to feed it. It was a problem. The seashore people weren't very *good* at catching fish. They liked to find their food sticking to the rocks. To catch fish you had to have a sharp beak and drop on them out of the air, or you had to swim *faster* than the fish and catch it in your teeth. But Pilp sometimes managed to catch a fish with his hands. Lisha could see him splashing wildly about in a low rock pool. He came back, grinning. In his hand he carried a wriggling little fish.

Lisha reached up for it. But no, Pilp wanted to feed the seal himself. He got into the water and held the fish out to the seal. But the seal didn't seem to know what to do with it. Too young to eat for itself. The little fish escaped and was glad to swim away into the seaweed.

'*Mummle!*' Lisha called her mother back. Mummle leaned over the edge of the rock. She was giving Swodge his breakfast of milk. He was getting a bit big for it and his teeth were growing, but seashore babies went on getting milk from their mothers for a long time.

'*Milk!*' said Lisha, pointing to the baby seal. She wondered why her mother suddenly looked quite cross. Perhaps she didn't have any spare milk. Oh well, Mummle seemed to have gone off the seal pup. Lisha would have to help it find its proper mother. But where?

'*Meeeeh!*' Sadly the little thing bleated again. It must be hungry.

What did its voice sound like? That sound which Lisha had heard in the night – the sad singing! That must have been the big seals. The wind had carried their voices. If she went upwind she might find them.

Seashore people knew all about the wind. You had to, because it was always playing tricks, and it brought the weather to you. There wasn't much wind today, but Lisha watched carefully to see which way the dark rain squalls blew across the flat water. She held up her wet finger. Which side felt coldest? That was the windy side. She must go that way, past the stack, round the point. What was there on the other side? She didn't know.

Better go, before anybody stopped her! She swam away from the rock. As she hoped, the baby seal followed after her – quite fast. It could certainly swim better than Swodge, and she was glad she didn't have to take it on her back! She was quite glad, too, to see that Pilp was coming with her again. There was a bark from Old Snoldge as they swam away, but they both pretended not to hear.

Seals

This was easier than yesterday, swimming through the flat sea. But she had no idea how far she had to go, so she took it easy. There, between her and the cliff, was the tall stack. The birds were quiet on this dull morning. There was the gap between the stack and the cliffs. When she thought of the leaping egg-robbers Lisha almost turned back.

Please, don't let me meet them again!

Who was she saying this to? To the sea, of course. If she stuck to the sea, it would look after her.

They were swimming alongside each other now, Lisha and Pilp with the little seal in the middle. It kept turning its dark eyes from one of them to the other, but it didn't seem to be getting tired at all. They had left the stack behind them, and there was the point now, a high ridge of land sticking out into the sea.

And, moving along the top of that ridge, black against the grey clouds – little figures!

Were they walking on four land-legs, or on two? It was too far away to tell. Lisha turned and swam out to sea, keeping well away from that point of land. Pilp and the seal followed her.

They were round the point now. Where was the land? There didn't seem to be any more! Not even a sand-dune. So where were they going? The flat sea seemed to have no beginning and no end. That distant seabird, was it floating on grey sea or flying in grey air? Which way should they go?

Then over the sad water they heard a sad sound. Voices rising and falling. And the little seal suddenly started speeding through the water, so fast that Lisha and Pilp couldn't keep up! He was swimming towards the sound of those voices. She followed as fast as she could, and so did Pilp. Surely a person as big as she was could go as fast through the water as a baby animal! It didn't even seem to be trying.

Ahead of them there was a long dark line above the water, with blobs on it. A long low island! The baby seal made for it. Lisha's feet touched bottom – it felt like fine shingle, little pebbles. The seal was ahead, humping itself on to the beach. But now it looked very clumsy and slow, and Lisha and Pilp were able to catch up with it.

The humps on the island raised their heads. Big seals, gazing with dark eyes. The baby made straight for them, bleating. But Lisha and Pilp stopped. They didn't seem to be needed now. The baby had found its family. And the big seals might not be friendly to people.

No! The big seals were pushing the little one away. Wrong family!

'Meeeh!' The little seal humped itself further along the beach towards some other seals. There were some babies there, but again the big ones drove the lost one away.

'Meeeh!' It was humping itself back towards Pilp and Lisha. Pilp made signs to Lisha to leave it there. But she couldn't!

She propped herself up as high as she could on Pilp's shoulders and looked round over the water.

Seals

There must be some more seal families somewhere. A long dark line over the water there. Humps on it, too. That was where the land ought to be, she thought. It must be the main beach. She splashed back into the water and tried to make a seal noise.

'*Maaaah!*' It came out differently, but the little seal was following her. The three of them swam towards the long beach. It wasn't very far, but the water got quite deep on the way.

They crawled out on to the shingly beach.

'*Meeeh!*' The little seal bleated. And a big seal answered, and started humping towards them. They met, kissed noses, and the baby straight away found its breakfast milk and was sucking away happily.

So *that* was all right! Pilp had already gone exploring up the low ridge of shingle, but Lisha stayed and looked round at these seal folk. They were plumper and smoother than her own seashore people. Their front and back flippers looked much better than her arms and legs for swimming with. Each one of them had a beautiful coat of fur to keep it warm. And their eyes looked clever and sad. She wondered if they could tell her the things she wanted to know – about the sea and the land, and *walking*.

'*Is it better to be sea people or land people?*' she asked.

They didn't seem to understand her words, but she looked into their eyes and, as if they had read the question in her thoughts, all the seals lifted their noses to the grey sky and began to sing.

The Seashore People

There weren't really any words to understand, so it must have been the music that told her what she wanted to know. And it came out something like this:

'We are the seal people.
We came from the sea, for all things come from the
*   sea.*
There were foes in the sea so we crawled on the
*   land,*
And fins became legs and we learned to breathe in
*   the air.*
There were foes on the land, we returned to the sea,
And legs became flippers again.
What are we now?
We stand in the sea and we look at the land.
We lie on the shore and we look at the sea.
Where do we belong?
This is our song.'

Lisha would have liked to hear more of their sad song. But what was Pilp doing, tumbling down the ridge of pebbles, shouting the alarm sound that Old Snoldge used?

'*Move! Move!*'

Was he playing tricks, just to break up the singing party? The seals were alarmed. As Pilp scrambled into the sea the seals followed him, with the young ones bleating and humping themselves after the big ones as fast as they could go. It was the sort of silly trick Pilp *would* play. Lisha wasn't going to take any notice.

But an uneasy feeling made her look over her shoulder.

And she saw! Over the shingle bank! A shaggy head. Two eyes looking straight at her. Ears, like hers, one on each side of the head.

She didn't stop to see more. She tumbled down the beach into the sea and dived down into the clear water. She held her breath and didn't come up for air until the bottom started sloping up towards the island.

All the seal families seemed to have hauled themselves up on to the island, but they were craning their necks up and looking at the land. Lisha looked back too. On the beach that they had just left, there were as many figures as she had fingers. Big ones, the size of Old Snoldge, but much skinnier. Little ones, Lisha-sized and smaller. Mother ones, carrying skinny babies on their backs. Every one seemed to have reddish-brown fur all over, bedraggled in the falling rain. On the pebbly beach they walked on their two feet, but they were always crouched over and often put their knuckles on the ground. Some of the big ones carried a rough stick in one hand.

The little ones chased each other up and down the shingle bank. A Lisha-sized one splashed into the sea and paddled in the water up to his knees. Was he coming across to the island? But no, none of them seemed to want to swim.

The middle-sized ones picked up pebbles and threw them. The seals were worried, and so was Lisha. But the stones landed with a plop in the water, not even half-way to the island. They went on throwing, just the same. It seemed to be a sort of game, throwing stones at the sea. Then they all wandered off along the misty shore.

I'm not really afraid of them, Lisha said to herself.

But on the long swim back to the home rocks she and Pilp kept well away from the shore.

4

WHALE

There was a storm coming from somewhere. All the seashore people knew it. There was hardly any wind in the bay, and no choppy waves out to sea. But the long, smooth sea-swell surged up and down on the rocks. One moment you could see the deep-growing weed that hardly ever showed above the water. The next moment the water washed over the dry rock, high up where you thought it couldn't reach you. When they reached the shore, the swells turned into great breakers that thundered on to the sand.

Feeding got difficult. Lisha and Pilp thought it was fun, riding up and down on the great surges, trying to grab a passing winkle. But there were not many shell-fish left on these rocks anyway. The people had eaten most of them.

'*Move!*' The short, gruff bark came from Old Snoldge.

He rolled himself to the edge of the rock and belly-flopped with a great *splosshh* into the water. In the sea he didn't look fat and lazy any more. He led the way, swimming with a strong, easy stroke. All the people followed. Where were they going? They didn't know, but they trusted Old Snoldge.

They didn't move fast. Mummle had Swodge to carry on her back, and some of the other mothers had even smaller babies clinging to them, and there were children younger than Pilp managing by themselves. It was fun, being on the move with all the people. You didn't notice the long smooth swells in the middle of the bay.

Lisha and Pilp played diving games. They ducked deep beneath the water and looked up at its sunny, silvery roof. It did look funny, all the people's legs flipping away above them! And strange sounds came to their ears down there.

Squeak! Grunt! Click-click-click. Pip pip pip pip . . . Where did they come from?

Lisha swam to the surface and took a breath. Up there she couldn't hear the sounds at all. She dived again to listen. This time the sounds seemed much nearer, and so loud that they hurt her ears. She went to the top again and looked out to sea.

Out of the sparkling water, smooth black shapes were leaping, curving over, diving back with a flap of flat tails. They were as many as the seashore people. And they were heading this way, fast!

Lisha swam quickly to Mummle and pointed them out to her. Her mother looked and smiled. She didn't seem to be worried.

Whale

'*Dolphins,*' she said.

The dolphin people sped up to the seashore people, turned aside, and swam along with them. Now they swam lazily, drifting with a wave of their tails, while Lisha and her family ploughed along with arms and legs at the same speed. There was a young dolphin swimming between Lisha and Pilp now, grinning and looking at them with its clever eye. What was Pilp doing? He was putting his arm round the smooth back of the dolphin – it didn't have a neck – and letting it drag him along! He was putting his leg over it and riding it! He was being carried along, sitting there half out of the water, riding the dolphin! But the dolphin needed to breathe. It arched to the surface, puffed and breathed in through the nose-hole on top of its head, flipped up its tail, and dived. Pilp tumbled off, and came up laughing and choking.

Lisha wanted to ride a dolphin! They had all sunk below the surface now. She went down to see what was going on, and her ears filled with a noisy chatter of dolphin-talk. *Squeak! Click-click. Grunt!* They were much more talkative than her own people, and Lisha had this strong feeling that they were *cleverer*. She felt a bit shy about riding on somebody who was cleverer than she was. But she wanted to ask them a question. What was it?

Too late, they were off! They suddenly shot ahead of the seashore people. Just an extra twitch of their tails and they were disappearing into the blue distance of the underwater world. Lisha came to the surface.

Her people were still plodding through the sea, but there they were, the dolphins, far ahead already, leaping up for their breaths of air.

She was sad that the dolphins had gone. *What's the use of being a seashore person?* she thought. *I can't go on two legs. I can't fly. I can't talk under water. And I can't even swim very fast.*

But she didn't stay sulky very long. She and Pilp went back to their diving games, swimming under other people and blowing lots of bubbles up at them. The underwater chatter of the dolphins had faded away ahead, but now Lisha was listening for anything else she could hear.

And what was *that*? That wasn't dolphin talk!

A long, deep, booming, wailing sound. It seemed to come from the deepest of the deep sea. From the deep, dark places that were even more fearful than the land was. Places where the seashore folk would not dream of going. Or, if they did dream, it was a bad dream. But who was making that sound, on this sunny day?

Pilp must have heard it, too. They both swam closer to their families after that.

They had crossed the mouth of the sandy bay. At the far end were a few low rocks, not at all like the high cliffs and stacks at the other end. And round this low point – what was there?

There was a different taste to the water, for a start. Not so salty, as if more raindrops had got into it. And there was a taste which she didn't know. It was something like the smell of crumbling rock high up on the

44

stack. A *land* taste – that's what it must be. Even the look of the water was changing now. It was more difficult to see through.

Lisha swam higher in the water for a bit, poking her head up to try and see the new shore. But even from the top of a big swell she could only see white breakers, not the shore they were breaking on. Old Snoldge was turning towards the white water. He wasn't leading the babies and children through *that* was he?

Now there were big white breakers on each side of them, but still the water was deep below them, and the waves they were swimming in were heaving high but not breaking. And then the water was even less salty, and on each side were flat banks of sand and mud. Old Snoldge led the way to a sandbank, and the tired people crawled out and rested.

'*Where are we, Mummle?*' Lisha asked.

'*River,*' said her mother, pointing away from the sea. Lisha wasn't sure what the word meant. It wasn't like any place she remembered. All flat sand and mud, with narrow waterways running here and there. Nowhere to play. And what was there to *eat?* She was hungry after that long swim.

After a rest, Old Snoldge called to the people and set out over an empty sand-flat. Some black-and-white birds were busy poking their long red beaks into the sand. But you can't catch and eat birds! Old Snoldge lolloped towards them and the people all followed, fathers and mothers, children and babies, scrabbling over the soft wet sand on hands and knees or hands and feet. Lisha and Pilp galloped ahead and made a race of it, though they weren't sure where they were racing to. The black-and-white birds flew up and away.

The grown-ups had stopped and were scratching with their fingers in the sand. Lisha and Pilp raced back again. *Shells!* People were digging up big round double shells, handfuls and handfuls of them, all growing together down in the sand.

'*What shells?*' Lisha asked her mother.

'*Cockles.*'

It wasn't easy to open them. No rock here to bang them on. No stones to hit them with. Some of the big people tried to crack them with their teeth, but they gave up.

But Lisha had noticed something in her play. In the bottom of one of the creeks she'd seen big flat stones. She galloped off again and found them, and held one up, calling to the other people. Everyone came and collected flat stones, and went back to the cockles – which were already trying to bury themselves in the sand again. They cracked open the shells between the flat stones, and they all had a cockle-feast, there in the middle of the sand-flat, with the surf booming a long way off. Then they stretched out in the sun to sleep it off. Very high overhead in the blue sky, white wisps of cloud were moving from the sea. Old Snoldge, lying on his back, seemed to be watching them carefully.

Whale

But Lisha and Pilp couldn't rest for long. They went off to explore the creek. There was hardly enough water to swim in, and it was so winding that you couldn't see round the corners. What were those gulls doing, wheeling and calling in the air over there? And what was sending waves along the creek – quite big ones? And what was that *thrashing* sound ahead?

They rounded a corner of the winding creek and – *what on earth, or what in water, was that?*

In front of their eyes a huge tail was thrashing up and down, beating the water into foam, and sometimes coming down with a loud slap on the sandy bank. It was a tail like the tails of those dolphins, flat, not up-and-down like a fishtail. But the tail itself was as big across as one dolphin!

Lisha and Pilp scrambled out of the water on to the sand. No room for *them* in the water with that thrashing tail! What was the other end like?

The creature's huge, wrinkled body filled the creek. On each side its flippers churned the sand. Air whistled painfully in and out of a breathing-hole in the top of its head, and there, near the end of its grimacing mouth, was an *eye*. The eye wasn't very big for the size of the body, but it was a big eye. And it wasn't stupid. That eye said a lot.

Lisha didn't need to ask anyone the name of this creature. Everybody knew the biggest thing in the sea.

'*What are you doing here, Whale?*' That was what Lisha wanted to ask that eye.

The eye looked at her. The great tail stopped

lashing, and the great fins stopped churning. And Lisha seemed to hear a voice. It did not come out of the whale's mouth, nor out of the breathing-holes on top of its head. It seemed to come from deep inside the great forehead. A long, deep, booming, wailing sound – the sound they had heard in the sea!

It had no words, for there were no lips to make them. But the deep wailing music seemed to say all this to Lisha:

'*I am Whale.*
We came from the sea, for all things come from the sea.
We crawled on the land and did well. On land we grew great.
Too big for the land! And so we went back to the sea.
And greater we grew. We are wise. We look after our young.
We dive to the depths for the food that we know will be there.
We circle the earth in the sea.
We carry within us our secret – the legs we don't need!
Only one thing we fear – and that is the land!'

Poor whale! Lisha could see the trouble in its eye. The mightiest of all creatures, on land or water – and helpless in a narrow sandy creek, left stranded by the sea. Did it even know what every one of the seashore people knew: that the water would come back to it?

Whale

She wished she could help by shoving it back to deep water. No, not all the seashore people pushing together could do that. Could they dig away the sand in front of it? No. Her people were too lazy. But the whale seemed to think she was a friend, and was calmer while she was there. It wasn't wearing itself out and hurting itself by thrashing at the sand. If she stayed with it until the water came back perhaps it would be all right.

Pilp, who didn't seem to care very much about the lonely whale, was up on the bank of the creek, looking out over the sand-flats. He suddenly pointed.

'*Look out!*'

He gave the danger call that Old Snoldge used. Lisha climbed to the top of the bank and looked.

A line of little figures was coming over the sand-flats from the land. It wasn't the seashore people. These walked on two feet, though their backs were hunched and some of them put their knuckles to the ground. And some carried rough sticks, and even used them to walk, like walking on three legs And Lisha was afraid now. It was the *land people!* And the safe, friendly sea was a long way away.

What would they do if they found her whale? What would they do when they met her people?

Pilp was galloping back to his family. He didn't care about the whale. Lisha thought she'd better do the same. But first she turned to the whale.

'*Keep calm. Wait for the water*,' she tried to tell it. Perhaps it understood. She left it lying there quietly.

The Seashore People

In the middle of the sand-flat, the land people were walking up to the seashore people. The fathers and young males of the seashore people had made a ring, and the mothers and babies were in the middle. The men were trying to look fierce. But they weren't very good at it. Seashore people were good at melting away in the sea when there was danger from land, or clambering on to rocks if there was danger from sea. They didn't know much about fighting. But what about these land people? They were strange – so they must be dangerous.

Lisha sneaked up behind her people and joined the circle. But she wriggled to the front. She wanted to see what was going to happen. The land people lined up and stared at the seashore people. The seashore people stared back. Nobody seemed to know what to do. And Lisha had an idea.

They had dug so many cockles that there were plenty left over from the feast. Lisha gathered up a double handful and pushed her way through the line of males. She had to walk on her knees. Holding out the cockles, she moved towards the land people.

Perhaps they were hungry!

Nobody said anything. Nobody moved. Then one of the land boys stepped forwards, and took a few paces towards her. Perhaps he was hungrier than the others. His grin seemed to be friendly. His fine gingery fur shone in the sunshine. He held himself up as straight as he could. He was *handsome!*

Lisha felt silly, down on her knees in front of him.

Whale

She was going to do that thing she hardly had a word for. She was going to *stand!*

She squatted. She placed both feet firmly on the sand. Very carefully, she straightened her legs. She straightened her back. She was standing!

She heard gasps and *Ooo* noises behind her. She tried not to wobble. The boy took a few more steps forward. Their hands touched as she tipped the cockles into his. Then the boy scampered back to his people – and Lisha fell over.

Now everybody knew what to do. The seashore people dug cockles as fast as they could. They showed the land people how to crack them with the stones – they just didn't seem to know *anything!* But perhaps they didn't like cockles very much. They soon started wandering off again over the sand-flats.

Towards the whale! What if they liked eating whale?

Lisha galloped back to the creek. She didn't wait for Pilp or anybody else. She had to get to the whale before those people did! There was a lot more water in the creek now, and she swam quickly. She couldn't hear the whale thrashing. Was it all right?

Round the corner – and there was the whale, lying calmly in a lot more water. Lisha got out on to the bank. There were the land people, wandering towards her. Ahead of the whale was a sand-bank. The whale still couldn't move forward. But beyond that was a deep channel, and sea-waves were moving along it. Lisha noticed that a wind had sprung up, and the sound of the surf seemed much nearer.

The land people saw the whale. They jabbered excitedly and started waving their sticks. She didn't think they could do much harm to the huge animal, but she hoped they wouldn't try. The whale saw the people. It didn't like them, and started thrashing its tail again. The people jumped back, away from that dangerous tail. They shook their sticks at the whale's head. Lisha stayed between the whale and the people. But nobody took much notice of her.

The whale was sploshing the water over the bank on to the sand. *No!* The water was coming from the sea! It was suddenly running all over the sand-flats. And the land people were alarmed. They were looking wildly round them, looking for the land.

Lisha slipped back into the deep creek and whispered to the whale, '*It's all right, the sea's coming back!*' It wouldn't be long before the water was deep enough for it to swim away. Now she could go back to her people.

But she heard the frightened wailing of the land people. Could she leave them here to – what was the word – *drown?*

She couldn't. She crawled out on to the sand-flat again. Young Ginger-Fur pointed to her. She beckoned, and set off over the flats towards the land. She didn't know this place any better than they did. But it was a seashore, and that was what she knew about.

Whale

The wind was rising, and so was the water. Crawling over the sand, she could move as fast as the others could follow, stumbling and splashing. There was a scream from behind her. She looked round. It was young Ginger-Fur, standing up to his waist in the water. He didn't seem able to move. What had happened to his legs?

She crawled back to him. *Quicksands!* They sometimes went like that. Sand so watery that you sank in it: water so sandy you couldn't swim in it. She pushed the boy over. Made him lie on his belly like her. Made him kick his legs free and crawl after her. Then she led the other people round the quicksands. If they *had* to stand upright, of course they would sink in.

Now the white breakers were driving her forward, but the land people were stumbling and falling in them. The day seemed darker. Looking up, she saw the sky covered with clouds. Even Lisha was fearful now. Where were her people?

Over the white water, a line of heads! There they were! And the sand was sloping up, and there was the dry rubbish of the high water mark under her hands. There were her people, squatting on the low shore, looking out for her.

And the land people ran whooping up and away in the land-weeds. No such words as *Thank you!*

But her own family were glad to see her. And all the seashore people huddled and cuddled together among the strange land-weeds, for a night of storm.

5

OTTERS

Everyone woke up hungry again. No breakfast snacks crawling about the rocks here. What did people *eat* on the land?

Old Snoldge was looking out to sea. The great white breakers were still pounding, far off on the sand-flats. The sky was covered with racing clouds and the wind whistled among the land-weeds. Old Snoldge gave a grunt and headed for the water of the river. Even here, choppy grey waves were running away from the sea.

Everyone followed. It was strange, plunging into this tasteless water. It didn't even hold you up as well as the sea does, and some of the smaller children found it difficult to swim. But they all got over to the other side of the river mouth, then Old Snoldge and the big ones stopped swimming. They were standing on the bottom – all right for them, but Lisha and Pilp and the little ones were left treading thin water.

Lisha clung on to Poppli. He was the man person

that Mummle spent most of her time with, and he was always quite nice to Lisha and little Swodge.

What had they stopped for? They all looked towards Old Snoldge. He ducked under the water and came up with – what was it? A stone, with two or three rough grey shells stuck to it.

It didn't look very nice, but Poppli and the other grown-ups were smiling and licking their lips.

'*Oysters!*' Poppli grunted.

The mothers with the smaller babies went to the rocky shore. Lisha and Pilp and the bigger children helped to gather the oysters from the bottom, diving among the grown-up legs and bringing the shells to the top. The grown-ups took handfuls of the shells, walked to the shore, and gave them to the women to crack open.

Funny! Lisha thought. *In the water, they're walking just like land people.*

Then they all went to the stony shore and had an oyster feast. Delicious! Whelk-and-winkle was all right for everyday food, and cockles made a change, but this was something special. Of course you had to be careful with the bits of broken shell in your mouth, and spit them out. Lisha's tongue felt something odd. Not a jagged bit of shell, but too hard to swallow. She sucked it. It was round and smooth. She spat it out into her hand and looked at it.

Pretty! A perfectly round, pinky-white little glowing ball, the size of her big toe. She showed it to Poppli.

Yes, he had a word for it. '*Pearl,*' he said. He

shrugged his shoulders and went on gulping oysters as Mummle handed them to him. But Lisha decided to keep the pretty thing. It didn't even go dull, as wet pebbles do. She held it in her hand and it seemed to glow even more as it warmed up. She showed it to Pilp and let him hold it for a bit. He threw it back to her. She didn't catch it, and it bounced off among the stones. She couldn't find it, and she was furious with silly Pilp. He helped her look for it, but it seemed that he couldn't find it either. Lisha turned her back on Pilp and sulked.

There was a splash behind her. What was he doing now? She looked over her shoulder. He was swimming away up the river. She wasn't going to let Pilp explore further than her. So she slipped into the water and swam off after him. She heard the usual warning bark from Old Snoldge – perhaps a bit sterner because they were going up the river. They both pretended to be diving for more oysters, but really they'd had enough of the rich food.

The waves were running up the river but the current was running out. You had to swim quite hard to move against it. A long way ahead, where the river got narrower, the land-weeds seemed to stand so *tall!* She wanted to go and look at them.

Birds flew from one side of the river to the other, over Lisha's head. Dark birds with floppy wings, and tiny little fluttering birds. They weren't at all like sea birds. And – *look there!* A little dark head popped up, not far in front of her, and two bright eyes stared at her.

Otters

A little seal? No, too small for that. It ducked smoothly under the surface, and a trail of bubbles showed that it was swimming towards the land. Lisha followed as quickly as she could. That thing wasn't going as fast as the dolphins did, but it was faster than she could swim. There it was again, popping up far ahead of her. It gave a whistling sort of squeak – and another whistling squeak answered from somewhere else. There was another little round head, over there! Now they were both swimming strongly towards the land.

There was a sound in Lisha's ears like the sighing of surf, but there were no big waves up this river to make such a sound. And it seemed to be coming from the air. She was much nearer now to those tall land-weeds. Were they making the sound? They grew on stiff stems near the bank of the river – tall as the stack where the seabirds nested, they seemed. And, yes, she could see land birds perching on them! The tops of these plants swayed in the air, as the great trees of seaweed sway in the surges of the sea. And yes, they made a sound like waves.

She followed the two little animals towards the land. What would they do when they got to it? Hump themselves up it like seals? Crawl on hands and knees? She gasped as the little things swam gracefully to a low beach – and bounded up the land without slowing down! They seemed to be just as happy on the ground as they were in the water. They raced up among some short green land-weed and began to play. Lisha swam as near as she dared to this strange land, and watched.

The two animals chased each other in circles, round and round in the weeds. They rushed up the trunk of a fallen tree and down a branch. They caught each other, and tumbled over and over, wrestling. One broke away, and played by itself. It threw little stones up in the air and caught them in its paws. Then the other one got up and plunged into the water. Now they were chasing each other in the water, swimming on their backs, rolling over and over, diving and leaving trails of bubbles. And then they dashed out of the water again and up the bank – and suddenly gave up playing and cuddled up together on the ground.

Lisha wanted to make friends with these little animals. She climbed up the bank, feeling very slow and clumsy, and crawled nearer to them. Suddenly, they had both popped upright on their hind legs, staring at her with their bright black eyes. They didn't wobble, they were firmly propped up by their long tails behind them.

'*Which side are you on – land or sea?*' That was what Lisha wanted to ask them.

They began a long, chittering, chattering song, both together, standing like that. This is what it seemed to mean to Lisha:

'*We are the otters.*
We came from the sea, for all things come from the
*   sea.*

Otters

We lived on the land, became nimble
We ran and we climbed and we tumbled.
But we stayed by the water and fished, for fish is
*   delicious.*
We catch what we can on the land, we catch what
*   we can in the river.*
Life's fun – both by land and by water!'

And then suddenly – *Whisk! Whisk!* They both shot off into the water again, and there was nothing to see of them but a trail of bubbles. Why had they run away? They hadn't seemed frightened of Lisha. Had something else frightened them?

Well, if they could go off into the water, Lisha could go and explore this strange land. Where was Pilp? There he was, in the water. He could stay there! He wasn't forgiven yet. Lisha set off, on hands and knees, over the soft green plants, towards the high trees. She was not in a hurry. Land was nicer than she expected. Some of the land-weeds had bright-coloured tips to them, and they smelt good. Little fishy things with buzzing fins swam through the air and stopped on the coloured tips. Here was a pretty air-fish with fins that were broad and coloured and fluttering. And there among the weed stems was a little creature crawling on hands and knees like her. Its skin was greeny-yellow and its eyes were on top of its head. *Hop!* It suddenly leapt out of Lisha's reach. *It's all right, I won't eat you,* she wanted to tell it.

Something else wriggled out of her way. A very

59

long thin land-fish, greeny-yellow too – with no legs at all. So you could manage on land without feet! But it wouldn't stop and make friends.

Lisha looked down at her knees. They were going green, where they had crushed the land-weeds. Was that all right? She wasn't turning into a land thing, was she?

The friendly sound of surf was nearer now – no, it was the wind in the high trees. Was it safe to go among them? They wouldn't fall over, would they? It looked dark in there, underneath them. But she crawled in. It was like diving deep among the tall seaweed forests, with the waves swirling overhead. And the smells were different here.

The wind overhead sounded like somebody laughing. Something bounced down on the ground in front of her. Something brown and shiny, and nearly round. She picked it up. *Pretty!* This made up for losing her pearl. She really would keep this one. She put it in her mouth and stowed it in her cheek. It tasted all right, but it was too hard to eat.

There was that strange laughing sound over her head again. Was that how the land-trees spoke? Something hit her on the top of her head and bounced off it. *Ooch!* It was quite a hard knock. What was it? Another of those brown shiny things. She found it and put it in her other cheek. Another fell, and another. She couldn't keep all of them! And there was more of that laughter up there. Were the trees teasing her?

All the time since the otters had left her she'd had

this feeling that someone was watching her, and now it was even stronger. She squatted up and looked round.

Another pretty land creature! A big one.

A pair of beautiful golden eyes, fixed on her. Sleek, smooth fur, that shone in the sunbeams coming through the leaves. Furry ears, pricked up. It stood strongly on four legs. And what big, sharp white teeth!

'*Who are you?*' Lisha wanted to ask. The big animal said nothing, and kept still – except for the tip of its long tail, which kept twitching.

'*What do you eat?*' was the next thing Lisha wanted to know. But still it was silent.

Did it eat otters?

Did it eat – *people?*

Could it swim?

How far away was the water? Why hadn't she stayed in it?

There was a rustling in the trees behind the animal, and it wasn't the wind. Something – it looked like a bit of dead wood – hurtled through the air and struck that long, twitching tail. The animal sprang round, spitting, and attacked the dead branch with teeth and claws. Lisha looked up at the tree. There was Ginger-Fur, the land boy, hanging by one hand and a hooked leg, grinning and waving furiously at her.

Quick – up in the tree! That's what the wave seemed to mean. But Lisha knew nothing about climbing trees. She couldn't move. The animal glared up at

Ginger-Fur, then back at her. It crouched low, and its paws moved up and down, feeling for a grip on the ground. The hair at the back of Lisha's head began to stand on end. She was afraid.

Thump! Another dead branch hit the animal on the rump. It turned again, snarling – and leapt furiously at the tree where the boy was chattering rudely at it. It was clawing at the bark, heaving itself on to the branch where the boy was hanging, crawling along the branch towards him!

But Ginger-Fur was just laughing, swinging to the end of the thin branch – and leaping over into the next tree! He was all right. He was much more at home in the trees than that thing with the teeth and claws was.

And Lisha knew where she belonged, too, In the water! But where was it? There were high weeds everywhere and she couldn't see through them. They stung like jellyfish, and scratched her with sharp hooked teeth as she blundered through them. Dust from the ground rose and choked her dry mouth. Was that noise the wild beast crashing through after her?

'*Lisha!*' That was Pilp's voice, calling. With a great effort she stood up and looked over the weeds. There was Pilp, squatting by the waterside!

She was half-running on her hind legs as she made her way out of the weeds to the bank, roughly pushed Pilp into the river, and plunged herself into the cool fresh water. She swam as fast as she could, out into the middle of the river, and Pilp seemed to feel her panic and swam with her.

Then she dared to stop and look round. Back on the bank, the beautiful, dangerous land beast was dipping a paw into the river, then shaking the water off. It was all right. Whatever it was, it didn't like swimming.

But Lisha and Pilp swam quickly back to the stony beach. Old Snoldge scowled at them. The people were just waking from their doze after the oyster feast.

Pilp took something from his cheek and held it out to Lisha. Her pearl. Lisha gave him one of her nuts. Friends again!

6

NEW MOON

The sun was going down the sky into the sea. From the home rocks, Lisha watched it sink. The warm air was so hazy that you could look at the sun without hurting your eyes. It looked huge and red. A dazzling red pathway led from the rocks to the skyline under the sun.

Now the sun was balancing on the hard edge of the sea. It bulged like a great red jellyfish and began to settle into the water. Now it was only half a sun. Its two edges were shrinking together. Now it was only a bright blip on the skyline. *Pop!* It was gone – and in that last second, the blip had turned green!

Lisha lifted her eyes to the sky.

'*Moon!*' she said, and pointed. Not far above where the sun had gone down, up where the pink glow turned into dark blue night sky, there she was, baby Moon, like a thin sliver of curved sea-shell. Moon hadn't been in the sky for quite a time. Now Moon had come back.

New Moon

Old Snoldge, sitting with his back against the rock that the sun had warmed, nodded to Lisha. He looked at the new moon and he spoke one loud word.

'*Move!*'

Old Snoldge humped himself to the edge of the rock and flopped in. Why did they have to move this time? There were no signs of storm. The sea was calm except for some little ripples that lapped half-way up the home rocks. And it was nearly sleeping time. But everybody followed. You didn't argue with Old Snoldge, or ask *why?*

Stars were coming out in the darkening sky. Round the rocks there was white lacy foam on dark water. Old Snoldge led the way out to the middle of the bay. The people followed, babies and all. Where were they going?

Not far. In front of them a thick pillar of rock stuck up out of the sea. It had a name, Lisha knew. *Moon Rock*. But it didn't look anything like a moon. It had a flat top, higher than the home rocks, and very steep sides. Old Snoldge led the way round to the other side. There were some boulders to climb out on to and some ledges and shelves that went up to the top. Puffing and panting, he got out and started climbing. Old Snoldge climbing! The families followed but Lisha and Mummle and little Swodge had to wait in the water for their turn to get out on to the rocks. There was Old Snoldge, right up at the top, barking at everybody else to hurry up. What was it all about?

The Seashore People

The older people helped the babies and children –
but Lisha and Pilp didn't want to be helped. The two
of them raced each other up, and flopped over on to
the flat top. It was almost like *land* here! There were
tufts of tickly land-weed growing.

At last all the people seemed to be up on the top
of Moon Rock. In the middle of them all, Old
Snoldge barked for silence. He was looking out over
the sea to where the sun had set, holding out both
his arms.

There was skinny Moon. It was her turn to sink
towards the sea, following the sun. She hadn't been
back long and now she was going away again.

Another sound came from Old Snoldge's throat.

'*Oooooooo! Moooooooon!*'

Old Snoldge was singing!

And all the people turned towards Moon, held out
their hands, and sang:

'*Ooooooo! Moooooooon!*'

The voices of the people sounded like the wind
blowing through caves in the cliffs. But it was a warm,
still night. More and more stars were coming out.
And Moon was standing tiptoe on the hard edge of
the sea. Lisha joined in the *Oooooo! Moooooooon!*
chorus and did her best to follow the song that Old
Snoldge sang. But she understood the music better
than the words, because Old Snoldge didn't have
many words. This is what they seemed to mean to
Lisha:

New Moon

'*Be with us, O Moon!*'

And the people sang:

    '*Ooooooo! Mooooooon!*
    Be with us!

For we are the People. We came from the sea,
For all things come from the sea.

    Oooooo! Mooooon!
    All things come from the sea!

Long ago we strayed to the land,
But the land did not love us.

    Oooooo! Mooooon!
    The land did not love us.

Woe to those who stray on the land,
For they shall be dried!

    Oooooo! Mooooon!
    They shall be dried!

We returned to the sea,
For the sea gave us life.

    Oooooo! Moooon!
    The sea gave us life.

O Moon, you lift up the rocks,
And your people are fed.

The Seashore People

Oooooo! Moooon!
Let your people be fed.

You lift up the rim of the land,
And the sea is not spilled.

Oooooo! Moooon!
Do not spill the sea!

Grow strong, grow strong, O Moon!
Be with us again!

Oooooo! Mooooon!
Be with us again!
Be with us again!
Be with us again!'

And the voices of the people wailed unhappily, because the sickly little moon was sliding deeper and deeper into the sea, until there was just one, thin bright spark left. And then that was gone. Now there was only the light of millions of stars in the dark sky, and lacy white foam on dark water round the rocks below. And, beyond the water of the bay, the sand dunes glimmered very faintly in the starlight.

Lisha wasn't comfortable, neither inside nor outside. The flat top of Moon Rock was crowded. The ground was itchy with land-plants, and she missed her favourite sleeping place on the home rocks. And she was feeling guilty. *She had strayed on the land.* She remembered the dry, dusty feeling of the thorn patches. She was lucky she hadn't been *dried!*

68

And it wasn't only dangerous, to go on the land – it was wicked!

She wanted to get away from the people and sort herself out. Now that the singing was over, why shouldn't she slip off into the dark water? She moved towards the ledges that led down off the rock – but a sharp bark from Old Snoldge called her back. He wasn't letting anyone go! But *why* not?

Lisha curled up sulkily at the edge of the rock and went to sleep. She dreamed a dream. She had wings and she was flying. She had feet and she was standing upright on pink sunset clouds. She had hands as well, and she was holding a huge, glowing pearl. No, it was the full moon! But her legs were weak and wobbly, and she had dropped the moon-pearl and it was falling into the sea, and she was falling towards the water herself and –

Splash! Not a very big splash. Just like a little wave wetting her. Where was she? She sat up. She was on the edge of Moon Rock, where she had gone to sleep high above the water. But she wasn't high above the water. It was splashing over the edge of Moon Rock!

How could that be? Moon Rock was higher than the home rocks. How could the sea have got up here? She looked across the water to the home rocks, but she couldn't see them. She looked towards the land, but she could see no beach. The sea seemed to be lapping at the bottom of the sand-dunes.

The flat top of Moon Rock was not quite level. One end of it was lower than the other, and this end was getting covered by the water. People were crowding up on to the other end, muttering and moaning. Was the land sinking away for ever? Would the water pour away over the rim of the land into – into *nowhere*?

The people were afraid, not of drowning straight away, because they could all swim. But they weren't fishes. They couldn't swim around for ever.

And Lisha felt worse than any of them. Perhaps it was all her fault, for straying on the land? Now all the rocks were sinking away from them.

But as the people huddled together at the higher end of Moon Rock, the rock seemed to stop sinking – or the water seemed to stop rising. At last Lisha went off to sleep again in a jumble with her mother and little Swodge.

When she opened her eyes again the bright sun was bouncing up over the sand-dunes. There was the broad beach below the dunes, all washed by the tide. But where was the water? She looked over the edge of Moon Rock, which was standing in a tangle of seaweed. Between it and the home rocks – no water at all! Well, yes, there were rock pools she never remembered seeing before, rocks she had only seen dimly under water, stretches of sand and pebbles she never remembered going on. More seashore than ever before!

All the people were waking up with excited cries, pointing out their new seashore. Even Old Snoldge was smiling. He didn't try to stop the young ones as they clambered down the ledge and slid down the slopes of damp seaweed. Lisha and Pilp were the first to get down. They splashed through the new pools and galloped over the new sand with all the other young ones – until they looked to see what the grown-ups were up to.

Breakfast! The sea had left behind a harvest of fresh seafood, which had been growing or living deep below the water. Crabs and lobsters, prawns and shrimps, whelks and sea snails trapped in rock pools, flounders floundering in sandy shallows. Lisha and Pilp found a pool of their own to hunt in. A fish face lurking in an underwater crack. Pilp put his hand in – then pulled it out quickly. Something had tried to bite him. The face came out of the crack, followed by body, yards of it, longer than Pilp's arm, longer than Pilp himself! A huge conger eel! They decided to leave it alone, and moved to a bigger pool, a dark pit in the sea floor. Lisha had to take a breath and dive to the bottom. Two eyes staring at her from a pallid jelly! Long arms reaching out to her! The whole creature crawling over the bottom towards her on many legs. *Octopus!* She shot up to the top and let that one alone, too. She and Pilp went back to their families, who were sharing out prawns' tails.

The gulls were enjoying their breakfasts too, all over the damp floor of the bay. One flock flew up, shrieking. What had disturbed them? Lisha turned to look.

People! The land people! Appearing over the rim of

the sand-dunes, sliding down them, poking along the very high tide mark at their base, spreading out over the damp sand in family groups. The seashore people drew together and glared at the others, invading *their bay!*

Some of the strangers were even wandering towards the home rocks! How *dare* they? Old Snoldge gave a growl. *Our rocks!*

Meeting these land people on the empty sand-flats had been bad enough. But now they were invading the seashore people's own rocks! Poppli and the men started galumphing over towards the home rocks. Was there really going to be a fight this time? Pilp scampered after them to join in the fun. Lisha followed, with an unhappy feeling in her belly.

She splashed through the new pools again and galloped over the wrinkled sand. They got to the rocks before the land people, who just stared at them as they wandered across the floor of the bay. The seashore people climbed up on their rocks. The slippery seaweed at the bottom was quite difficult to climb. The rocks themselves were beautifully sea-washed and clean, even the sleeping cave. But the land people didn't seem specially interested in them.

Except one! He was trying to climb up the weedy base. *I might have guessed,* Lisha thought. Of course it was Ginger-Fur.

Ginger-Fur didn't like the seaweed so he moved round to where the rock was bare. Using tiny cracks and crevices for hand-holds and toe-holds, he was climbing higher and higher. Lisha moved along a ledge to watch him. Such a clever climber! Lisha wished she could climb like that.

There was a growl from the top of the rocks. What were her people doing up there? She looked up.

At the top the rock was looser. Pilp had rolled a big lump of rock to the edge, right over where the land boy was climbing. The others were smiling as he looked down at Ginger-Fur and got ready to drop the rock on his head.

'*NO!*' Lisha screamed.

She was nearer to the land boy than she was to the rock and Pilp. She couldn't stop Pilp dropping it. Instead she hurled herself along the ledge, below Pilp and above the climbing boy.

Whooosh! The rock fell past her ears – Pilp had done his best to miss Lisha. It bounced off the slope near the boy, sending a shower of bits all over him. He lurched, missing a hand-hold and foot-holds. He was hanging by one hand.

Lisha reached over the edge of the ledge, held out her hand to him, and pulled him up on to the ledge, on to Home Rock.

He squatted there, and Lisha sat up close to him. Her people up above wouldn't drop any more rocks while she was there. He had saved her from the wild beast. She had saved him before, from the quicksands. But it was strange, having him so close to her. He smelt quite nice, warm and furry. His eyes were *blue!* His teeth were white when he smiled at her.

The Seashore People

Below them, the sea was beginning to creep back over the floor of the bay, and the land people were hurrying back to the dunes. They weren't going to be trapped again! Ginger-Fur made a move to join them, but Lisha moved with him, keeping close all the way down the rock and over the seaweed.

They parted where the lacy foam was washing over the sand. Ginger-Fur went off over the dunes with the land people. Lisha went back to her rocks.

7

FULL MOON

Lisha woke up on the home rocks. Was it daylight? No, Moon was in the sky, full and round, shining on Lisha's face. She couldn't go back to sleep.

Old Snoldge had made the people sleep at the very top of the rocks that night. Now Lisha could see why. The land had sunk deep again. Not quite as deep as at the time of the new moon, but the bay was very full of water. Over there was Moon Rock, low in the sea. She looked across at the sand-dunes. She could see them as clearly as if the sun was shining, but there was no beach below them. The small waves seemed to be breaking at the foot of the dunes.

What *was* over the other side of the dunes? *Nothing?* Were they just a rim to stop the sea slopping over? Perhaps. But surely land was more than that? She had seen it, been on it, met land creatures. She wished she could meet them again.

Moon stared down at her. Was Moon telling her to stop her wicked land thoughts? Moon didn't seem to be telling her anything. Moon was just shining as bright as day. And Lisha couldn't sleep.

All the other people were sleeping: Mummle, Poppli, little Swodge, Pilp, her uncles and aunts and the other families, even Old Snoldge. There was nobody to stop her.

Stop her doing what? Doing what she wanted to do – to see what was on the other side of the dunes.

Very carefully and quietly Lisha rolled herself to the edge of the rocks. Hanging on with her hands, she lowered herself into the sea. Just to make sure nobody could see her go, she took a deep breath and swam away under water, under the mirror surface silvered by the moon.

She came to the top in the deep water of the bay, breathed again, and swam quietly towards the shore. She felt for the sandy bottom with her feet. Still out of her depth. The dunes looked very close, very white in the glare of the moon. The one eye of the moon stared down at Lisha. Perhaps she ought to turn back now?

But a wave suddenly dumped her on to the steep beach and she crawled forward straight into prickly land-grass. Might as well keep going, up the slope of shifting sand, only held together by grass roots. The sand wasn't sun hot, it was moon cool. It was hard work, climbing upwards, even worse than going up rock ledges. She was grasping rough plants in her sea-soft hands, hauling herself higher. *Aaah!* – that one had painful spines! It hurt! But she had to get to the top, whether it was wicked or not.

Full Moon

Nearly there! She stopped to get her breath back. She'd rather swim all day than climb like this. She lay back and looked at the sea. Sparkling silver ripples shone below the moon. There was black Moon Rock in the middle of them, and there were the home rocks where her family lay sleeping. How beautiful it all was, and how friendly – *her sea!* Did she really want to look at the land?

Well, she was only going to look, and then go back. Nobody need even know. One more struggle, and she would be at the top.

But she wasn't at the top yet. The dunes were higher than they looked, though it wasn't as steep at the top. Lisha crawled onwards and upwards.

Then – there was the land in front of her. So *much* of it!

Lisha didn't have words for what she could see from the high dune. The ups and downs of the sand-dunes went on and on. In the hollows were shadowy clumps of low trees. Then flat stretches of stiff land-plants growing out of water. So land wasn't all dry, Lisha thought. Yes, and over that way was a long ribbon of water winding its way into the land. Was that the river she had gone up with Pilp? There were trees and trees and trees! And then the land went on getting higher again, and there were rocks on the land! And, far in the misty distance, much *much* further than Lisha had ever looked in her life, the land stuck up in huge sharp points that blocked out the stars. The land was – it was beautiful too! In quite a different way from the sea.

The Seashore People

Who lived on all that land? Perhaps as many creatures as lived in the sea?

Hop! – something leapt out of a grass clump and went running and jumping down the slope away from her. Her heart went *hop* too! What was *that*? Quite small, and in the moonlight she could see its little bobbing white tail. It was afraid of her, whatever it was. She wondered why.

'*Whooo? Whooo?*'

Her heart jumped again! There was a rush of air past her ears and a bird swept over the dune. Its broad wings were silent and Lisha saw neither neck nor beak. She tried to watch its flight over the moon-lit hollows and dark thickets.

One of the hollows was bigger than the others and had a broad flat floor to it. Figures were moving round this floor, figures Lisha thought she had seen before! They were moving round and round like gulls circling in rising air, or like an eddy of foam where the sea runs through rocks. They moved, each on two feet, and they held each other's hands. Oh yes, it was the land people. But what were they doing in the moonlight?

Lisha had to go and see. She went along the tops of the dunes, sliding down sand-slopes and clambering up the peaks again, getting nearer to that hollow but not trusting the shadowy thickets. She only meant to *watch* those strange people. Up here she could still turn and look at the friendly sea. She wasn't going down on to the land. As she got closer she could hear sounds. Singing! Not the wailing sounds of her people's moon songs. More like the *akkety-awk, akkety-awk* of the birds, only more together. And there were tapping and rattling sounds, like people banging things, that went with the singing.

But when Lisha got to the nearest tall dune she could see nothing of the hollow. It was hidden by the top of a lower dune. She could hear very well though. The music got faster, and there were hoots and happy laughter. What *was* going on? She would just have to go down and see.

She slid down a long sandy slope. At the bottom the plants and low trees grew thickly. She would have to crawl through them. She tried to keep quiet, but dry leaves rustled beneath her hands and knees, and dry sticks cracked. Perhaps it didn't matter. The people were making so much noise themselves. They wouldn't hear.

She forced her way through a tangle of twigs – and she was out in the moonlight before she expected it! There she crouched, on the sandy, grassy floor of the hollow, with the moon shining full on her, and the suddenly silent land people all round her.

She couldn't move. But some of the bigger, shaggier land people moved to pick up sticks and stones. They stood round her in a half circle.

Only one thought helped Lisha in her terror. *They're afraid of me too*, she thought. *They don't know what I am or where I've come from*.

The females and young ones had been pushed to

the back, away from this monster that had sprung out of the thicket. But a smaller figure was pushing between the grown-up legs, and crossing the open space between her and the sticks and stones. She didn't recognize it at first. In the strong, pale moonlight its fur shone like gold. But it was Ginger-Fur all right. He bent over her and looked into her face. She could see his white teeth smiling. He turned away and jabbered something to the others. Some of the big ones jabbered back. But Ginger-Fur seemed to be getting his own way.

And it was all right now! Lisha was one of the party! But she still wished she'd had the sense to run away.

The younger ones crowded round her. Small furry females stroked her long hair and patted her bare skin. They were all being nice to her, but she wished they wouldn't. They brought her food and she felt she ought to try it. Nuts, cracked open. Not bad! Eggs to suck. Gone off! The girls giggled as they held out to her flabby white round things on fat stalks. Lisha nibbled at these too. They tasted like the smell of the forest floor. They brought her drink, in a big sort of land shell hacked open at the top. It foamed and bubbled like surf round the rocks. They lifted up the shell for her to drink, and all laughed when it made her choke and cough. *Disgusting!* But it was too late to spit it out.

And now the rattling of sticks and the clashing of stones and the *akkety-awk, akkety-awk* singing

Full Moon

started up again, and they were grabbing Lisha by the hands, and *pulling her up on to her feet!* And, held up like that by hands on each side, she was spinning round in a circle like the rest of them on the floor of the hollow.

Or was it the moon and the stars that were spinning madly round above her? Or was it just her head spinning? Because her head was making words of the singing and chanting, and it went something like this:

> 'We are the people!
>   The people!
>   The people!
> Ours is the land!
>   The land!
>
> One can be weak,
> Two can be feeble
> Together we stand!
>   We stand!
>
> Feet on the earth,
> Earth is our birth.
> See the big sea!
> One day we'll swim it!
> One day we'll fly!
> Sky is the limit!
> Bright is the moon.
> We'll be there soon!'

But it was all too much for Lisha. She spun off out

81

of the dance and tumbled on to grassy turf. The moon and the stars wouldn't stop spinning over her head. Her stomach turned over inside her, and everything she'd eaten and drunk came up on to the ground.

She'd got to get home! How could she get back up and over those tall sand-dunes? She crawled off through the grasses, hoping nobody would notice she had gone. Yet she needed help! She didn't think she could manage it alone.

Lisha never remembered much about that climb up the dunes. But there was someone helping her, giving her a hand up the steep banks of loose sand, and looking anxiously in her pale face when she had to stop for breath. It was the boy she had always called Ginger-Fur.

But when they did at last get to the top the sight of the moonlight on the calm sea revived her. The two of them sat for a while, listening to the peaceful *sshushhh* of the waves on the one side, and the raucous noise of the land folk on the other.

And they exchanged their real names.

'*Yakku*,' said the boy, tapping his chest.

'*Lisha*,' said Lisha shyly, pointing to herself.

Then she started off down the slope towards the sea. That was easy enough now, but Yakku came all the way down with her. When they reached the edge of the surf he looked anxious again. Would she be all right, alone in all that water?

Of course Lisha knew she'd be all right. She plunged in, and as soon as the cool water buoyed her up all her dizziness and tiredness left her. She turned to wave to Yakku standing lonely there on the sand, golden in the moonlight. He waved back, and she turned and swam off to the rocks.

She swam gently, thinking about those strange land people. And what a strange song! If she'd got it right, they had been singing about things that hadn't even happened yet! Lisha hadn't got a word for time that hasn't happened. And was there a word for standing on your feet and spinning round? How could she tell her family what she had been doing?

But when she got back to the rocks nobody stirred, not even Old Snoldge. None of the seashore people had even noticed that she had gone away. She quietly found her usual sleeping place and fell into a deep sleep.

But she had this funny dream.

There was this sunny beach. It was like the beach she knew, but it was covered with people! So many people that you could hardly see the sand! Was there that number of people *in the world?* Some of the smaller people were crawling around on hands and knees in the usual way, piling up heaps of sand as Lisha sometimes did. Some of them were in the sea, swimming among the waves – but not swimming very well. Most of the bigger people were doing what big people normally do, lying in the sun, dozing. But a lot of the younger ones were on their feet, racing about, hopping in and out of the waves, running away from the breakers as if they were afraid of them!

The Seashore People

All the people had long hair on their heads, some longer than others. They had smooth bare skin, though some of the men had hairy chests. But what were those funny scraps of colour they all seemed to have, stuck on their tops and bottoms, all except the very youngest?

And why was Lisha, in her dream, especially interested in two little people? One was Swodge-sized, with fair hair: the other was a bit bigger, and gingery. They were toddling off towards the sea, hand in hand.

In the dream, someone beside Lisha was calling out, 'Not too near the water!'

And Lisha was saying, 'They're all right. They're *my* children!'

And the person beside her was saying, 'They're *mine* too.' And it was Yakku!

What a silly dream! Lisha woke up on the rocks, laughing. The early morning sun shone on the empty sea and the empty beach.

It was quite a nice dream, though!

8

FRIENDS

It was hot on the rocks. They could burn you if you touched them. Lisha found a shady crack and sat in it. She watched to see if the rock was rising out of the water. The sea was so calm that you could nearly see it happening. Every day the rock rose and fell, rose and fell. A funny thought came to Lisha. Perhaps the rock stayed still and the *water* moved up and down. Was it wicked to think like that? She looked at the shady place where Old Snoldge usually lay on very hot days. What would he think?

But of course, Old Snoldge wasn't there any longer. There had been new moons and full moons, new moons and full moons since she had seen Old Snoldge, but she couldn't get used to him not being there.

She knew what had happened to him. He had just got tired on one of the long swims, tired of being the leader of the seashore people. And he'd gone back to the sea. It was all right. He was all around in the seawater now, still with them. He had sunk wearily into the deep sea and become part of it. Part of the sea, from which all things came. *For all things come from the sea.* Even the land people must have come from the sea at some time.

Tap. Tap. Tap.

The sharp sound came clearly over the water. Was it a gull trying to break a shell? Lisha peeped out of her crack. She could see no bird on the home rocks.

Tap. Tap. Tap.

It came from the middle of the bay. There it was – it was Otter, Big Otter, lying on his back in the smooth water, with a flat stone on his belly. On the stone lay a big seashell, and with his forepaws Otter was holding a rounded stone, using it as a tool to crack the shell and get the meat out. Otter was so *clever!* Perhaps he would teach Lisha how to crack shells on her tummy. Perhaps he would play with her.

She slipped into the warm water and swam towards Otter, who was munching his shellfish. But Otter flipped over, dropped his flat stone, and was gone below the surface. He didn't seem to want to be friendly.

Lisha looked around over the water. Wasn't that Otter, further over in the bay? She swam towards the round head and the two sad eyes that were gazing at her. But it wasn't Otter, It was Seal. And Seal sank gently down and disappeared too. He wasn't being friendly, either.

Lisha turned over on to her back and swam lazily.

Friends

The sun dazzled her eyes, so she covered them with her wet hair and it made rainbows. She did a water-trick, diving over backwards, pulling herself under with her arms and flipping her toes up towards the blue sky so that she sank into the green depths. You had to blow air out of your nose all the time when you did it or the water would get up it when you were upside down.

Pip pip pip pip. Click-click-click. Faintly, from a distance, she could hear underwater dolphin talk. She rose to the surface and took a breath. Looking out to sea towards the sun, shading her eyes with her hand, she could see dark shapes leaping smoothly out of the water and in again with a sparkling splash. She wished she could play with the dolphins, but she knew she could never catch up with them. She wasn't quick enough in the water to make friends with dolphins.

She dived down to listen again. What was that long, deep, booming, wailing sound, fainter and more distant than the dolphin talk? Was Whale out there too? She surfaced and looked out again. Yes, *there!* A humped back above the water, a spout of watery steam, a great tail slapping down. Whale was sailing past, near the horizon, on his important business. Whale was all right. Did he remember who had saved him from the land? She would like to get to know Whale again, but he was too big to play with.

Lisha turned on her back again and kicked lazily with her legs. The back of her head and her shoulders grounded on the sand. She had reached the beach. She lay there with the little waves lapping over her legs, eyes shut, too dreamy to do anything more.

Akkety-awk! Akkety-awk! Akkety-awk! Why did those birds have to make so much noise? What were they doing, hovering in clouds over the beach and diving down to it? They were supposed to fish in the sea, not on the land.

Something small tickled her neck. Something else was wriggling under her armpit. And was that another one in her wet hair? She opened her eyes and sat up. What *was* going on?

She combed the thing out of her hair with her fingers. She didn't like things in her hair. What was it?

It was much smaller than the palm of her hand in which it lay, kicking its four tiny flippers and goggling at her with two little black eyes. Lisha knew what it was. It was one of Mother Turtle's babies. They must have hatched out in the hot sand.

She looked up the beach. Yes, if she looked carefully she could see a line of little crawling turtles, dragging themselves through the loose dry sand, almost skipping along where the damp sand was firmer, and tumbling head over heels in the wavelets of the surf. But they all seemed to know where they were going. To the sea, which none of them had ever seen.

And of course the gulls had seen them too. That was why they were hovering and diving. Dinner was on the beach. Lisha watched a bird standing on the sand trying to get one down. It seemed to be a tough, leathery morsel even for a gull.

Friends

It wasn't fair! Soon there would be no baby turtles left. She felt sorry for anything that lived in the sea and crawled on four legs like herself.

Shhh! Shhh! Lisha hissed at the birds. She picked up pebbles and hurled them towards the birds, but she wasn't very good at it.

Awk! Awk! Awk! The birds screamed at her crossly. But they kept on diving down. Silly birds! How would they like it if something ate their eggs? Oh, well, things did eat their eggs, and they didn't like it, but that didn't stop them eating turtles. What could she do to protect the little four-legged things?

She could make a little river to help them into the sea. Something to dig with? She looked around the beach. Half a scallop shell lay in the wet sand. Hadn't she used this one before, some time?

Little rivers of salt water were trying to get back to the sea. If she joined them all together the little turtles could swim down faster and the gulls wouldn't get them. She dug channels, slanting across the sand slope. They collected the water and the water collected the little turtles and swept them into the deeper river she was making, where they swam with the swift current towards the sea.

No more turtles were coming. She followed the last ones into the surf. They didn't stop to play or say thank you. They had disappeared into the great sea, and Lisha was alone again. And all that digging had made her hot. She lay in the surf as she had done before, on her back with her feet towards the sea.

The Seashore People

High, high overhead, thin white clouds moved over the blue of the sky. Or was the whole sky toppling, gently spinning above her? Her ears were full of the murmur of waves. She closed her eyelids and the sunlight shone red through them.

Ow! Something damp and scratchy landed on her bare belly!

A crab! A dead smelly crab! She threw it off.

She sat up, twisted round, brushed the hair out of her eyes. Where had it come from?

There was a line of footprints leading away – with big spaces between them. And yes, there was a figure running up the beach, and the sound of a laugh coming back.

She didn't have to guess, though it was only a back view. It was Yakku. Did he want to be friends? But who wanted friends who put dead crabs on you?

She wasn't going to take any notice of him. She was quite happy playing alone, wasn't she? She crawled back to her little river and began to build a dam to stop the water flowing to the sea. She kept her back to Yakku, pretending he wasn't there, but she knew he was up to something, further up the beach.

The water was flowing down and filling up the pool she had made.

No it wasn't.

It was rushing down the sand a bit further on, missing all the channels she had dug for the turtles. She knelt up to see what was making it do that. It was Yakku. He was digging furiously with a bit of driftwood, cutting off all the water from her river and sending it somewhere else. When he saw her looking, he grinned and waved at her.

Well, she could dig a channel and make the water come back! She quickly dug one out to where the water was running away, and turned it back into her pool. It captured quite a lot of other trickles too, and a lot of water was flooding in. She had to work hard to keep her sea wall going, and to dredge the sand from the pool to make it deeper. The little puddle was becoming a swimming pool.

She was working so hard, digging with her shell and scooping with both her hands, that she hardly noticed someone else working with her now. Yakku had got the idea, and was making channels and rivers and canals, all leading to the pool.

She had to scoop more and more sand out of the pool to make room for all the water. But where could she put the sand? She dumped it in a pile, higher and higher. Now Yakku was in the pool with her, scooping out sand and heaping it up. It was a big heap now, but it wasn't very *pretty*, Lisha thought. She looked around for little coloured shells and stuck them on the sides of the heap. Yakku looked puzzled, but he scampered about and brought more shells, and fine seaweeds, green or red. Lisha stuck them on, she knew where they ought to go. But Yakku found a beautiful white gull's feather and stuck it on top.

Lisha had got very hot and sandy after all that work. She lay down in the pool to cool off, and so did

Yakku. But it was too shallow there for Lisha. She climbed out and crawled into the sea, until she was far enough out to lie there with her nose just above the surface, and she could feel the sand washing off her.

She raised her head and looked back at Yakku. He was standing in the sea with the water just over his ankles, looking at it doubtfully.

'*Come on in!*' Lisha called, and beckoned.

Yakku took a few steps. The water came up to his shins.

'*Come on! It's not cold!*' Lisha called, and waved.

Yakku didn't look happy. But he took a few more steps forward and stood with the water over his knees. The sea was very still. It just heaved a little bit. Lisha floated there quietly on her back. When she looked round again, Yakku was standing up to his middle. He looked so *silly!* How could he ever learn to swim if he kept standing up?

Lisha took a breath, turned over and swam beneath the water towards Yakku. It was not very clear, so near the beach. But there were his legs, standing stiffly there. It would be *kind* to give him a swimming lesson. Lisha knocked Yakku's legs forward and he fell over backwards under the water. Anyhow, that paid him out for the dead crab!

But anyone would think she had tried to drown him! He struggled and thrashed about, trying to get his legs back. She helped him up and he stood there gasping and choking and coughing, with seawater streaming out of his nose and mouth. Lisha was quite alarmed. Should she have done that? Was he very cross?

Yakku got his breath back, saw her looking anxiously at him — and he was laughing! He splashed Lisha with a lot of water, and she pretended to be upset, and fell over backwards herself. And Yakku actually let himself fall forward in the shallow water and tried to swim like she did. He swallowed a lot more water, and Lisha tried not to laugh at him. What was the land people's song?

See the big sea!
One day we'll swim it!

Yakku had a lot to learn first!

And it was only then that Lisha and Yakku noticed that people were watching them. They weren't alone on the beach.

A hairy bunch of land males were squatting halfway down the sand-dunes, pointing at them and wagging their heads.

And further up the beach some seashore fathers were wallowing in the surf, glaring across at the land men. Lisha could see Poppli among them. Poppli was their leader, now that Old Snoldge was gone.

What was going to happen?

Yakku looked towards the land people and made a move as if to run back to them. But Lisha grabbed his arm. No, they must face this together.

The Seashore People

A group of land females came sliding down the dunes. Some of them were carrying babies, or leading toddlers by the hand. Yes, even quite small land people could walk! They took little notice of the males, and went on down to the tide line and rummaged among the jetsam left there by the high water. And from the sea came swimming seashore mothers, Mummle among them with Swodge on her neck. They crawled to the edge of the surf and lay there cooling off and scrabbling for buried shellfish.

Perhaps she had better go back to Mummle, Lisha thought. But Yakku pulled her back. He didn't want her to go.

And now there was a pack of land children, up to Yakku's size and bigger, charging down from another part of the grassy dunes, whooping and leaping towards the surf, daring each other to put their toes in. And Pilp and his friends, boys and girls, were splashing out of the water and squatting in a group, staring at the land children.

Lisha was sure she'd never seen so many people on the beach – *yet she got this strong feeling that, yes, she had.*

It was her dream! That was it. Everyone on the beach together! And it looked more like a dream beach than a real one because – they had hardly noticed before – a great black cloud had covered the sky, but the sun peeped under it and lit up the figures on the sand. Yet the air was as hot and heavy as ever.

The land people had set up piles of flat pebbles,

and were throwing round pebbles at them to knock them over. The sea children had crept up on the other side of the piles, to watch the game. There was Pilp, trying to throw stones like a land boy, but not nearly as good. This was a game that Lisha and Yakku could join in. They moved towards the pebble piles. On one side were the sea children: on the other side the land children. Playing together – but playing apart. An uncomfortable feeling in Lisha's belly told her that the game might go wrong.

Someone was crying among the sea children! A stone from the other side had gone too far and hit a young girl. Lisha saw Pilp, scowling, pick up a stone and throw it as hard as he could back at the land children.

The game *had* gone wrong. She had to stop it! She hurried through the surf – almost *running!* But what was she going to do? Stones were flying from both sides, and they were hitting people! And – worse and worse – land males were hurrying to join in, picking up bits of driftwood as they came. And Poppli and the sea fathers were advancing the other side. It would be a battle!

Then – a sudden flash of light, like bright seaweed jumping from the black clouds to the sea!

BUMP! – RUMBLE RUMBLE RUMBLE
rumble rumble rumble rumble!

And sharp little pebbles of frozen sky came hissing

down into the sea and bouncing on the sand. The beach was swept by the stinging hailstorm. All the land people were racing up the dunes and disappearing over the top, looking for the shelter of the woods. And the seashore people were diving for the shelter of the sea.

Yakku splashed to the beach and ran off after his own people. Lisha sat in the sea, covered her head with her arms, and watched him. Her friend was gone.

But half-way to the dunes, Yakku turned and waved.

'*See you!*' Lisha shouted, and waved back.

She heard Yakku's voice.

'*See you!*' it seemed to say.

She had still got a friend. Lots of friends, perhaps. Some day *all* the people would play together on the beach, and it wouldn't be a dream.